From: carrenwoods@comcast.net
Sent: Monday, April 21, 2014 10:28 AM
To: Charles Fraga
Subject: Follow Up

Charlie,

Thanks for the tea and time to meet last week. It was wonderful to learn a bit more about you and your journey. Hope you had a wonderful Holy Week, and feel renewed and refreshed for the days to come.

I went through some of the articles that were written about the book Best Friend Tree, and have included some for you to have. I also will include a letter written by the Associate Pastor, who oversaw all the various ministries, at Beaverton Foursquare Church.

"Best Friend Tree is a beautifully written and illustrated book for children (of all ages). It would be a wonderful gift."

"The illustrations are great! A touching story not just for kids!"

"Best Friend Tree is a book for all ages. The story and illustrations touch the child in all of us."

One newspaper review said: "The story is based on Sandy's life growing up in a children's home in Portland. Although it was written for children, the book has great appeal for adults."

The Hospice Chaplain that used it on their house calls shared stories of being able to read the book as a way to share the Gospel with the people they met. One woman accepted Jesus as her Savior because of the book, and she knew she was dying, and so she had it put in her will that the book was to be saved and then given to her young daughter when she was 12 years old along with the letter the mother had written. In the letter she told her daughter how the book changed her life forever, and that she wanted her daughter to read it, and know that it was the reason for her hope, peace and comfort.

One father shared that he needed another book because he had to read it every night to his daughter, and it fell apart, so he was given another book. His daughter even took the book to bed with her every night for over a year.

There are many more stories and newspaper articles about the book, but hope that gets you started. If you need more, just let me know.

Here is the letter from Chuck Updike of Beaverton Foursquare Church:

"Best Friend Tree" is unique as far as books go. It is a children's book cleverly illustrated with brightly colored pictures and a story so simple that a small child can follow it. But, it is also a poignant auto-biographical sketch of a small girls experience with loneliness and her finding of a true friend.

*The author has created that rarity in children's books. A story that children delight in and adults enjoy reading.

Sandy herself is a highly skilled artist and a very accomplished teacher of children and adults.

The Lord Jesus (her best friend) has done a marvelous work of redemption in her life and the lonely little girl is now a source of joy to all who know her.

I strongly recommend the book which I have given to all my children (for my grandchildren), but I am even more pleased to recommend Sandy, my friend, who is a real joy to my life.

I also have another letter from Ron Mehl, Pastor at Beaverton Foursquare.

Charlie, I will get you a copy of the other book she did that was published by Multnomah Press. Sandy said that they returned the rights to her, so it would be available to be republished. She would like to redo the illustrations before it is published again. She was on a very tight timeline the first time, and isn't satisfied with all of the drawings, but most people would think they were wonderful:-)

Thank you for being willing to see where the Lord may lead us on this journey.

Blessings,

Carren

BEST FRIEND
TREE

Written and Illustrated by
Sandy Gunderson

BEST FRIEND TREE
Published by Thumbuddies
15615 SW Jaylee St.
Beaverton, Oregon 97007

Printed in the United States of America

Library of Congress Catalog Card Number: 94-90253
ISBN: 0-9642070-5-2

DEDICATED TO MY
BEST FRIEND
TREE
AND TO
CHILDREN OF ALL AGES

BEST FRIEND

TREE

ree stood in the big yard at the Children's Home where he had stood for more than fifty years. He watched the children playing on the playground across the long driveway which ran past his post in the yard. Tree had watched many children come and go over the years, but there was one who was very special to him; a little girl with curly hair and big brown eyes.

She was only four years old when they met. She came to see him almost everyday. Sitting on the ground beneath him, she would lean against his rough side or would sometimes lay on her back looking up at his huge branches. They enjoyed each other's company very much.

T ree would spread out his branches full of beautiful green leaves to shade her when it was hot. He would catch the raindrops so the Little Girl would not get wet when it rained. The raindrops would play a special song on Tree's leaves and all the birds would come and sit on his branches and they would join in the song.

pit pat

pit pat

tic tic tic

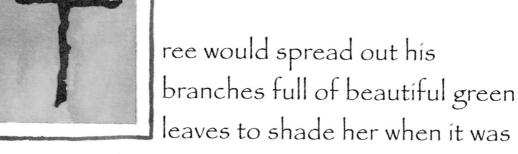

he Little Girl loved that song. It would make her feel warm inside and she would sing it whenever she felt lonely. She would sing it at night to make herself fall asleep.

They spent hours together. Tree would watch as the Little Girl would sit beneath his branches playing with "stick people," grasshoppers and stones. She would watch the birds in Tree's branches looking down at her looking up at them!

e listened as the Little Girl would tell him about important stuff; like how her snowman picture was chosen to go on the board outside the door of the kindergarten room and how she got to draw the church for the Thanksgiving mural in her classroom and she showed him the clay bird she had made.

oon little wings would begin to fly down. She called them whirlybirds. The Little Girl loved watching them twirl their way down to the ground. Sometimes they flew away on the wind like the birds, farther than she could see.

She loved Tree in the winter because she could look up through his bare branches and watch the clouds racing by. They were always in a hurry to get somewhere.

She loved Tree in the spring because his branches would get little bumps all over them. She knew it would not be long before Tree would show his new leaves that he had hidden all winter like a secret.

She loved Tree in the summer because his leaves were big and green and the sun would peek through the leaves looking like diamonds sparkling down on her.

She loved Tree in the fall when his leaves would turn a beautiful gold and he would let go of them and drop them on the ground for her to lay on, run through and crunch. It didn't make her sad when they all died and fell off because she knew a secret . . . he'd grow new ones in the spring. He always did!

When she took them to school her teacher told her they were seeds that would fly off on the wind and land somewhere. Then they would bury themselves in the ground and die and begin to grow. It was like Tree had little trees somewhere, even if she couldn't see them.

hen she would see other trees that looked like her best friend Tree, she wondered if it grew from one of his seeds that flew away on the wind.

ne day the Little Girl came to
say she had to go away. She
hugged Tree and tried hard
not to cry. She did not come back. Day
after day Tree waited . . . day after
day, week after week, year after
year . . . the Little Girl did not
come back, but still Tree
watched and waited.

ow, on this cool day in November, Tree stood in the big yard where he had stood for over 50 years still watching; still waiting. Today was different somehow. He felt it in the air. He watched every car that came up the driveway that day.

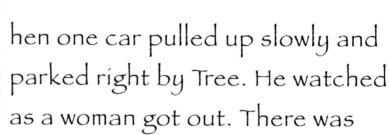hen one car pulled up slowly and parked right by Tree. He watched as a woman got out. There was something about her . . . She looked up with such sadness. "Tree?" she almost whispered. It was her! After all these years! It was the Little Girl. She was taller and so was he, but it was her!

h, Tree what happened to you?" she said. One of his large branches had been cut off since she had seen him, and a disease had eaten a large hole in his side, but in spite of the gaping hole, Tree still stood as majestic and straight as he had when he was younger.

h, Tree I've missed you so much," she said, "but I never forgot you! And look!" She held up the clay bird . . .

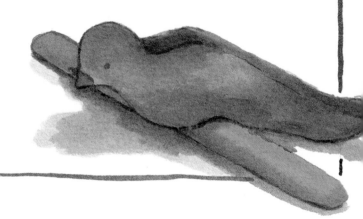

She told Tree about the years since she had gone. She told him about another tree she had heard of that stood long before she and Tree were here . . . It wasn't a tree with leaves that died in the fall, but it had a man on it that died for everyone in the world. She told him how they put Him in a tomb, just like putting one of Tree's seeds in the ground when it died, but it didn't take as long for new life to come to the man as it did to the seed. In only three days He walked out of the tomb . . . alive!

nd she told Tree that she had learned a song from this man and this tree too. "Would you like me to teach it to you?" she asked. His few leaves seemed to rustle a little in the wind in reply. So the Little Girl, now grown, sat once again under Tree. As children played on the playground nearby, and Tree listened, she began to sing softly . . .

esus loves the little children . . .
All the children of the world . . .
Red and yellow, black and white . . .
They are precious in His sight . . .
Jesus loves the little children
of the world . . .

And Tree too!